My Bum is SO CHEEKY!

Dawn McMillan

Illustrated by Ross Kinnaird

SCHOLASTIC

My bum is so *cheeky*!

It's unruly and wild.

I need a new bum!

A bum with manners.

A bum that is mild.

Jumping and **BUMPING**.

Behaviour so **bad**.

My bum is **ridiculous**!
My bum acts like a **fool**.
It causes trouble
when I go to school.

The morning goes well.

Until ...

there's a bad smell in Show and Tell.

The classroom's a **riot**.

The teacher wants quiet.

Everyone goes ...

'Pooooo!'

'That smell came from yooooou!'

My bum is a **rascal**,
so hard to restrain!
It likes to **jump** puddles
and play in the rain ...

Get my trousers **dirty**,
worn out and **tattered**,
leaving my folks feeling
worried and shattered.

A problem indeed! My folks think I need
some quiet time to sit down and read.
Or … to watch a TV show for a bit.
My bum might relax if it has to sit.

So ...

My bum starts to slouch, here on the couch.
On fluffy cushions, the cushions that slump.
Cushions just right for a bum that goes

bump.

And on the chair where Dad sits at night.

Yes ...

My bum and Dad's chair fit together just right.

So possibly ...
My bum will *chill*. I think it will.
I think it might settle and stay very still.

But ...

A square bum is **interesting**.
A square bum is **rare**.
A square bum fits perfectly
down the back of a chair.

So here I am with my legs in the **air!**

My mum is laughing.
My dad is too.
And then they do what they need to do ...

Pull!

And luckily ...

My **cheeky** bum is completely intact.
It's all round again and it still has a **crack**.

It's ready to jump. It's ready to play.

And guess what I've found in our yard today ...

My birthday present! A new trampoline!
It's the best present I've ever seen.

My bum is so happy. It's great at seat drops.

One then another, the fun never stops.

Seat drops with half twists, five at a time.

My bum's a natural! Its balance is fine.

Now my bum has ambitions.

My bum is **bold**.

About the author

Hi, I'm Dawn McMillan. I'm from Waiomu, a small coastal village on the western side of the Coromandel Peninsula in New Zealand. I live with my husband Derek and our cat, Lola. I write some sensible stories and lots of crazy stories! I love creating quirky characters and hope you enjoy reading about them.

About the illustrator

Hi. I'm Ross. I love to draw. When I'm not drawing, or being cross with my computer, I love most things involving the sea and nature. I also work from a little studio in my garden surrounded by birds and trees. I live in Auckland, New Zealand. I hope you like reading this book as much as I enjoyed illustrating it.

Published in the UK by Scholastic, 2022
Euston House, 24 Eversholt Street, London, NW1 1DB
Scholastic Ireland, 89E Lagan Road, Dublin Industrial Estate, Glasnevin, Dublin, D11 HP5F

SCHOLASTIC and associated logos are trademarks and/or
registered trademarks of Scholastic Inc.

First published in New Zealand by Oratia Media, 2022

Text © Dawn McMillan, 2022
Illustrations © Ross Kinnaird, 2022

The right of Dawn McMillan and Ross Kinnaird to be identified
as the author and illustrator of this work has been asserted by them under the Copyright, Designs and Patents Act 1988.

ISBN 978 0702 31378 3

A CIP catalogue record for this book is available from the British Library.

Printed in Italy
Paper made from wood grown in sustainable forests and other controlled sources.

1 3 5 7 9 10 8 6 4 2

This is a work of fiction. Names, characters, places, incidents and dialogues are products of the author's imagination or are used fictitiously. Any resemblance to actual people, living or dead, events or locales is entirely coincidental.

FSC
www.fsc.org
MIX
Paper from
responsible sources
FSC® C023419

www.scholastic.co.uk